nickelodeon

DORA the EXPLORER

Dora Goes to School

Turn the page
to learn with me
and my very best
buddy, Zee!

adapted by Leslie Valdes
based on the screenplay written by Leslie Valdes
illustrated by Robert Roper

Based on the TV series *Dora the Explorer*™ as seen on Nick Jr.™

SIMON SPOTLIGHT/NICKELODEON
An imprint of Simon & Schuster Children's Publishing Division
New York London Toronto Sydney New Delhi
1230 Avenue of the Americas, New York, New York 10020
For information about special discounts for bulk purchases, please contact Simon & Schuster Special Sales at 1-866-506-1949 or business@simonandschuster.com.
Manufactured in the United States of America 0712 LAK   This Simon Spotlight edition 2012 2 4 6 8 10 9 7 5 3   ISBN 978-1-4424-4948-0
This book was previously published, with slightly different text.

In this book, you will learn to . . .

✓ **READ** with us

 MOVE with us

 SHARE and CARE with us

✓ **DISCOVER** with us

 **CREATE** with us

 **EXPLORE** with us

✓  **COUNT** with us

 MAKE MUSIC with us

Hey there! I'm Moose and this is Zee. We're so glad you picked up this book today. We can't wait for you to find out what happens in this story!

It's the first day of school—hooray!
The students *y la maestra* are on their way.
But when *la maestra* Beatriz's tire goes flat,
Dora and Boots rush to help her, just like that!
To get to class they must count and sing.
Will they make it before the school bell rings?
It's a letters and numbers adventure for Dora.
Read this book and be a school day explorer!

Check out the last page for an alphabet activity you can share with your friends!

Dora and Boots were on their way to school. They were excited for their first day!

As they were walking along, however, they saw someone else on the way to school too. It was their teacher, *la maestra* Beatriz!

La maestra Beatriz needed to get to school before her students, so she could get everything ready for them and welcome them to class. But her bicycle just got a flat tire! Dora and Boots needed to help her get to school, and fast!

"*La maestra* Beatriz has lots of school supplies, Dora," Boots said. "How are we going to carry them all?"

"Backpack can carry them," Dora said.

So Boots and Dora helped *la maestra* put all her supplies in Backpack.

"Now we need to find the quickest way to school," Boots said.

"Who do we ask for help when we don't know which way to go?" Dora asked.

"Map!" Boots cheered.

Map told Dora and Boots that first they needed to go through Letter Town and over Number Mountain to get to school.

"Letter Town, Number Mountain, and School. Let's go!" cried Dora.

"We need something that can take us through Letter Town really fast," said Boots.

"Look, Boots!" said Dora. "*El autobus* can take us through Letter Town fast! *¡Vámonos!*"

"Dora, there are letters everywhere in Letter Town," Boots said. "We need to follow the letters and sing the alphabet song to get through town," Dora told him. "Let's sing!"

Dora and Boots sang the alphabet song, and before they knew it, they were on their way to Number Mountain.

All of a sudden, Boots heard a bell ring.

"That's the second school bell," Boots said. "We have to hurry!"

"We just need to find Number Mountain," said Dora.

Boots looked around. Then he saw a pink and purple mountain with numbers all over it.

"Look, Dora! There it is!" he shouted. "There's Number Mountain!"

"Great looking, Boots!" Dora said. "Let's go!"

"We need to get over Number Mountain fast," said Boots.
"Our friend Azul the train can take us over the mountain fast,"
Dora said. "*¡Vámonos!*"

"To ride over Number Mountain, we need to count the numbers we pass," Dora explained. "Let's count, Boots!"

"One, two, three, four, five, six, seven, eight, nine, ten!" they both counted happily.

"*¡Excelente!*" said Dora. "Now let's count backwards as we go down the other side. Ten, nine, eight, seven, six, five, four, three, two, one! *¡Fantástico!* We made it over Number Mountain."

Dora and Boots were getting closer—they could even see their school. But they still needed a way to get across the forest. Suddenly, Dora saw her animal-rescuing cousin, Diego!

"Wow, Diego's flying on a condor," said Boots. "Maybe the condors can fly us to our school."

"Good idea, Boots!" Dora said. "Let's call to the condors. Say 'Squawk, squawk!'"

So Dora, Boots, and *la maestra* Beatriz all squawked as loudly as they could to call over the condors.

The condors soared down and gave everyone a ride through the air right to the school. "Thanks, condors!" Boots said with a smile. "¡Gracias!"

"We made it to School!" Dora cheered. "Quick! Before class starts, we need to check Backpack for *la maestra* Beatriz's school supplies!"

Boots helped Dora check Backpack. "Pencils, chalk, notebooks, and rulers. We have everything we need!" Boots said. "*La maestra* Beatriz is ready for class to begin!"

But just then Dora heard a noise. "Uh-oh!" she said. "I hear Swiper! That sneaky fox will try to swipe *la maestra's* school supplies. We have to stop him!"

Dora and Boots stood tall and said, "Swiper, no swiping!"

"Oh Mannn!" said Swiper. He snapped his fingers and scampered away.

And just in the nick of time too! *La maestra* Beatriz's students began filling up the classroom.

"Good morning, class," *la maestra* Beatriz said with a smile.

"*¡Buenas días!*" said her students.

La maestra Beatriz was happy to be able to start her class on time. And she couldn't have done it without help from her star students, Dora and Boots!

Dear parents,

We hope your child enjoyed this Dora adventure. To extend this story, have a conversation with your child about it. You can ask what her favorite part was and why. Or have her tell you what she is looking forward to on her first day of school.

This book is also a great starting point for talking to your child about the importance of the alphabet and letters. Remind her how Dora and Boots sang the alphabet song to get the bus through Letter Town. Here's an alphabet activity your child will enjoy doing with you, using materials found in your home.

A Is for Alphabet. Let's Make an Alphabet Scrapbook!

From your friends at Nickelodeon and Simon Spotlight

1 Take thirteen sheets of paper and fold them in half to make a book. Staple the middle to keep the pages in place.

2 Label each page with a letter of the alphabet.

3 Together with your child, decorate each page with pictures and letters from magazines or newspapers that correspond to each letter. You may also encourage your child to draw and color her own pictures. Be creative! Use stickers, markers, crayons, glitter, etc.

4 Once her scrapbook is complete, have your child show family and friends what she has created. Maybe she can even bring it to school for show-and-tell!